IF YOU CALL MY NAME

IF YOU CALL MY NAME

by Crescent Dragonwagon   Drawn by David Palladini

Harper & Row, Publishers

If You Call My Name
Text copyright © 1981 by Crescent Dragonwagon
Illustrations copyright © 1981 by David Palladini
All rights reserved. No part of this book may be
used or reproduced in any manner whatsoever without
written permission except in the case of brief quotations
embodied in critical articles and reviews. Printed in
the United States of America. For information address
Harper & Row, Publishers, Inc., 10 East 53rd Street,
New York, N.Y. 10022. Published simultaneously in
Canada by Fitzhenry & Whiteside Limited, Toronto.

First Edition

Library of Congress Cataloging in Publication Data
Dragonwagon, Crescent.
    If you call my name.

    Summary: As she contemplates being with someone
special, a little girl imagines turning into a
fish, a hawk, and a lion.

    I. Palladini, David.   II. Title.
PZ7.D7824If 1981   [E]   78-22480
ISBN 0-06-021743-X   AACR2
ISBN 0-06-021744-8 (lib. bdg.)

For Ned Shank, who called my name

If the fish calls my name, I may go.
I could be eating breakfast,
I could be finding my books for school,
but I may go.

I would run the road in my running shoes
shoes that shine fins as my feet and legs turn to tail
down where road meets sea
where I answer the fish, crying

                              fish fish fish it's me!
And he is a silver fish
and I am a silver fish
turning girl to fish as I slither silver into the water,
my truest home,
home where I move like the sound of waves
home water moving my tail and fin

like a flag being moved and blown by the wind:
we the two slick sleek fish who flash through seaweed,
under the bottoms of far boats with triangle sails
two silver fish down where Coke bottles catch the light
into green glass jewels.
We don't talk.
We don't laugh.
Our flowing fishbodies sing silent songs
and the bright green eye he flashed at me
is enough.
I may go if the fish calls my name.

If the hawk calls my name, I may go.
I could be kicking one gray stone along,
keeping it on the sidewalk.
I could be sitting quietly in the dark under the house,
where the dusty boards are piled up,
but I may go.

Throwing my clothes into the air
running running running the path to the meadow
my shoes turn to wings
my dress a slim feathered body
my hat a sharp birdhead all above me
and I leap up and into my birdbody
girl to brown hawk I'll be, crying

                        hawk hawk hawk it's me!

And two brown hawks fly
where the yellow sun is warm on our open wings,

moving brown circles through the bluest sky,
our truest home,
home for brown feathers,
how we arrow the air and sleek and smooth our strokes,
home with one wingstroke
we simply soar—
calling to each other with no words but our own
and the bright black eye he flashed at me
is enough.
I may go, if the hawk calls my name.

If the lion calls my name, I may go.
I could be taking a bath,
thinking my own thoughts
mounded by bubbles in the hot water,
but I may go.

The yellow towel that dries me
softens and grows to a thick yellow coat
and my wet hair grows to a yellow unbrushed fur
and my tail springs up
and I pad and leap on my thick strong paws
girl to lion I'll be, crying
                    lion lion lion it's me!
And we two are stalking
in quiet perfect strength.
And the very air bends to our noble passing.

Everything seems quiet for us

passing through chinks of sun that the thick trees let through,

passing in dark jungle

rich with vines and fruit and greenness

the deep green dark our truest home

where we may roar or not, as we decide

where our big cats' eyes can see as clearly in shade as sun

where the bright yellow eye he flashed at me

is enough.

I may go, if the lion calls my name.

But if you call my name,
I will go.
I might be sleeping under a red quilt,
but if I hear the pebbles you throw against my window,
I will go.
And me with you I will be
mitten and glove, hand to hand, snow-running, crying
                              you you you it's me!

And on the beach we see boats with triangle sails
rise and fall far
and thinking of two silver fish
we stamp our names in snow on the wintery beach.
Walking back along the road sometime in spring,
we might stand suddenly still and holding our breaths
see, at the same moment,
two brown hawks circling above us, then flying away.

If we walked in the woods,
and it was fall,
if we sat leaning against the same tree,
our legs stretched out in front of us in the dry leaves,
sharing an apple bite to bite,
you'd touch my arm to be quiet,
and the wintery trees would turn green and leafy,
and be suddenly filled with bananas and coconuts
and drooping hissing snakes.

Bright birds would fly,
and you and I
would see the two:
the lions, strong and yellow,
silent on their graceful paws.
And we would talk or laugh,
or we might not.
But your bright blue eyes would flash at me,
and that's enough.

And if you call my name, I'll go.